The Night Before Christmas

GOLDEN® and GOLDEN & DESIGN®
are trademarks of Western Publishing Company, Inc.

A GOLDEN® BOOK
Western Publishing Company, Inc.
Racine, Wisconsin 53404
No part of this book may be reproduced or copied in any form
without written permission from the publisher. Produced in U.S.A.

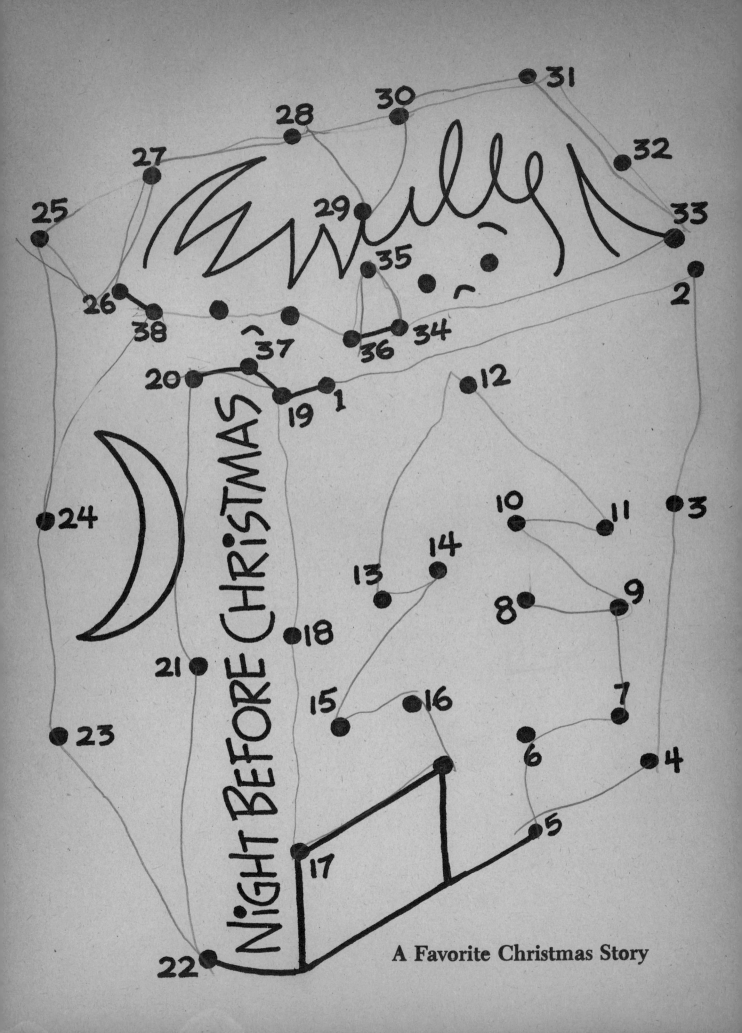

NIGHT BEFORE CHRISTMAS

A Favorite Christmas Story

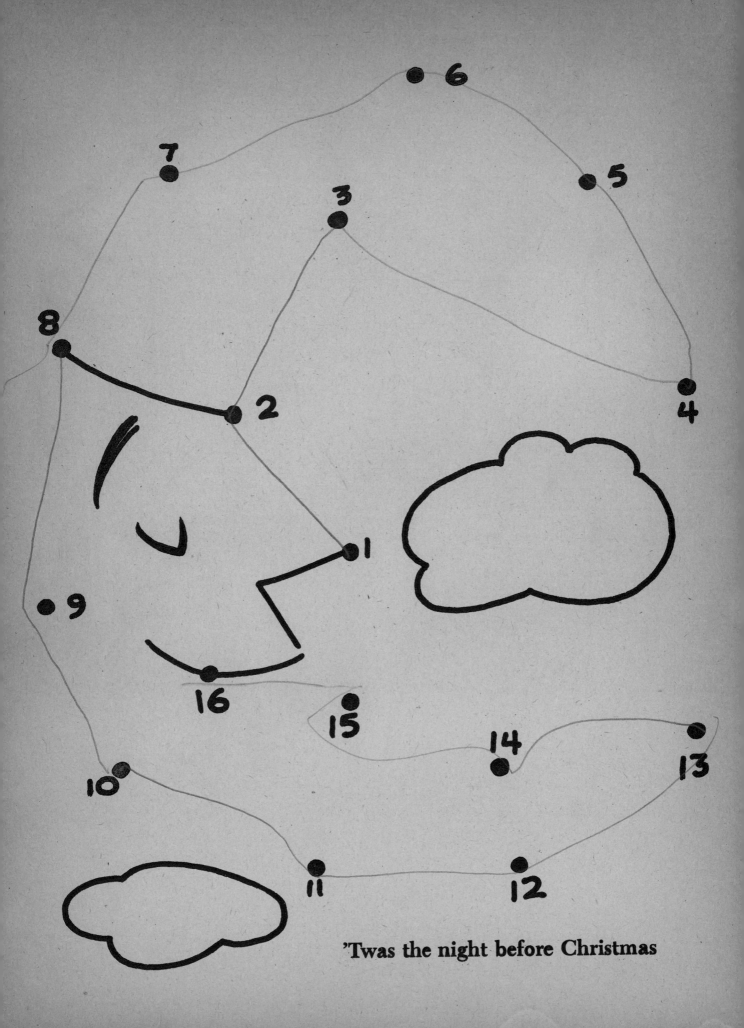

'Twas the night before Christmas

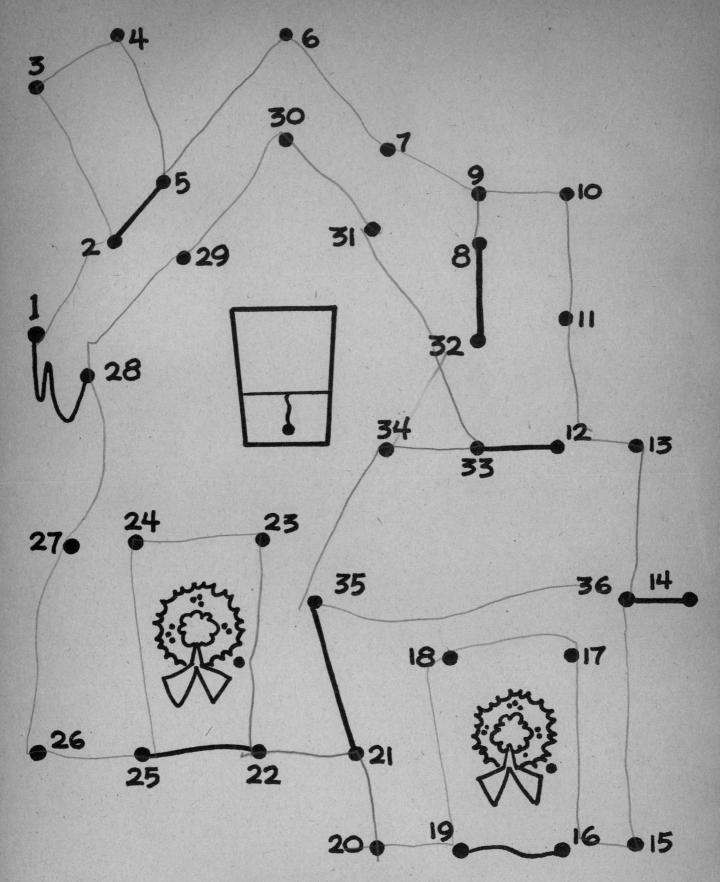

When all through the house
not a creature was stirring,

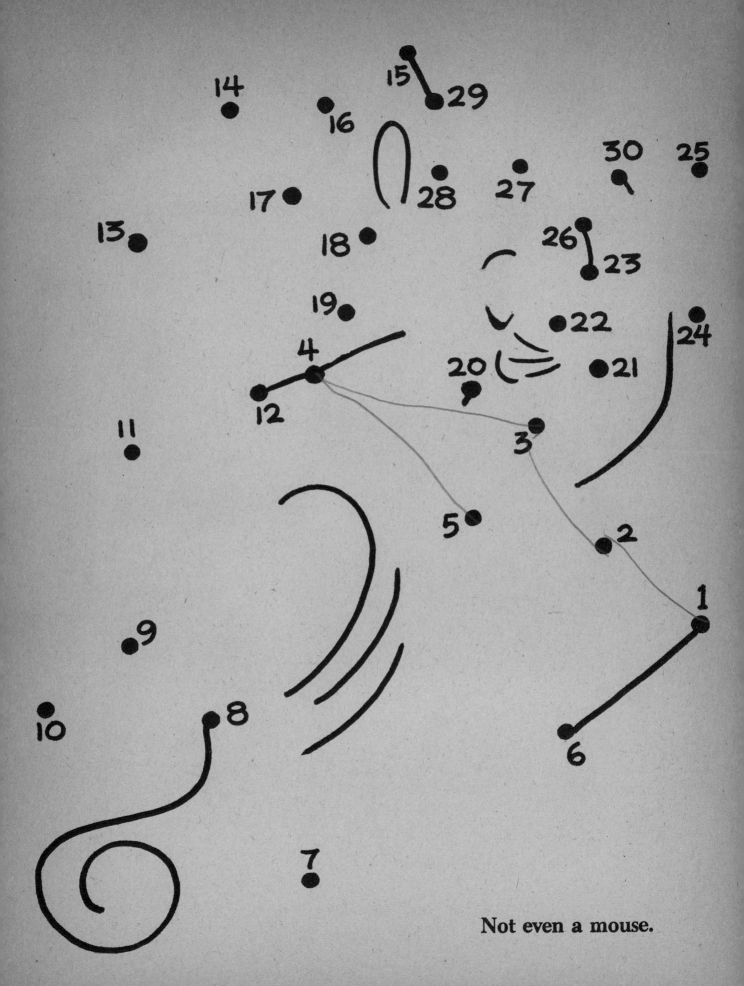

Not even a mouse.

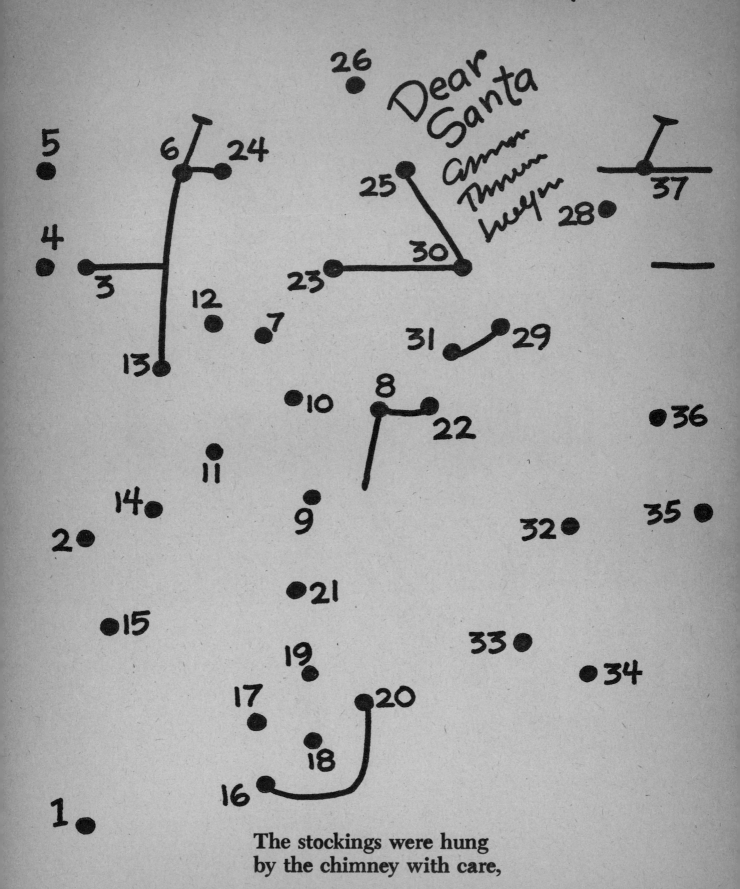

The stockings were hung
by the chimney with care,

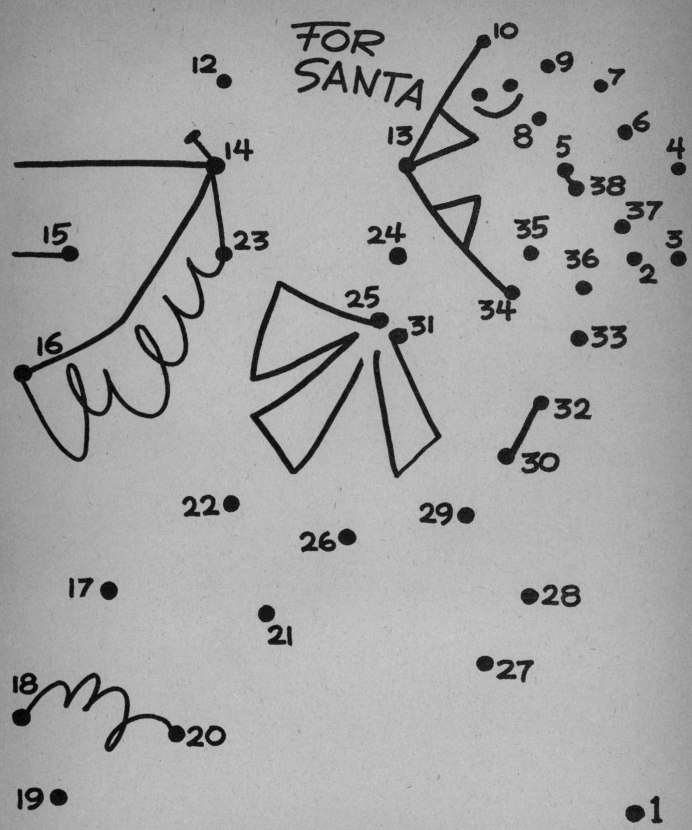

FOR SANTA

In hopes that Saint Nicholas
soon would be there.

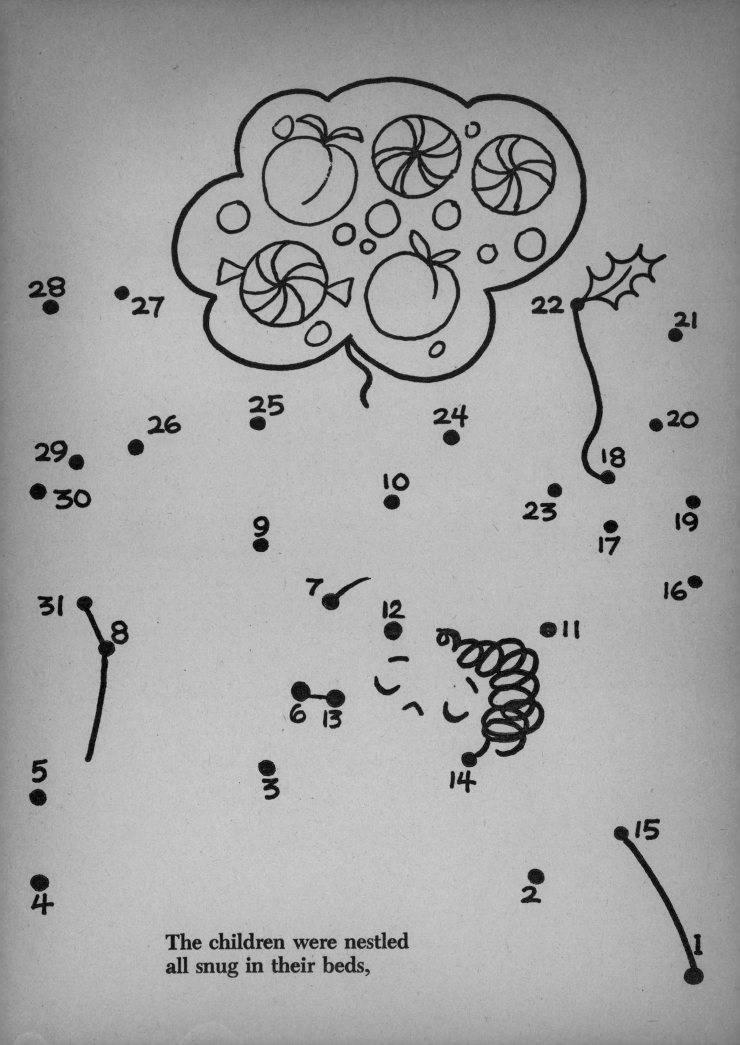

The children were nestled
all snug in their beds,

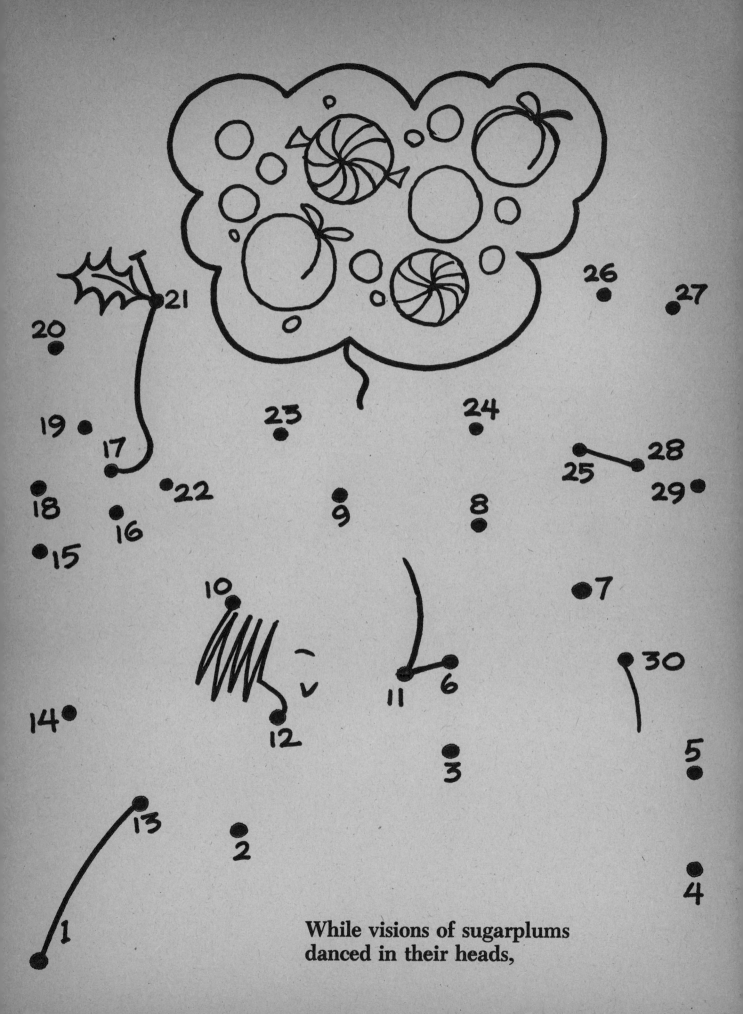

While visions of sugarplums
danced in their heads,

26

24● 23

28 25

29

8

27 9

11

7 10 22

5 21

6 2 12

30●

1

31 4 13

20

3

14 19

17

32 18

15

16

And Mama in her kerchief

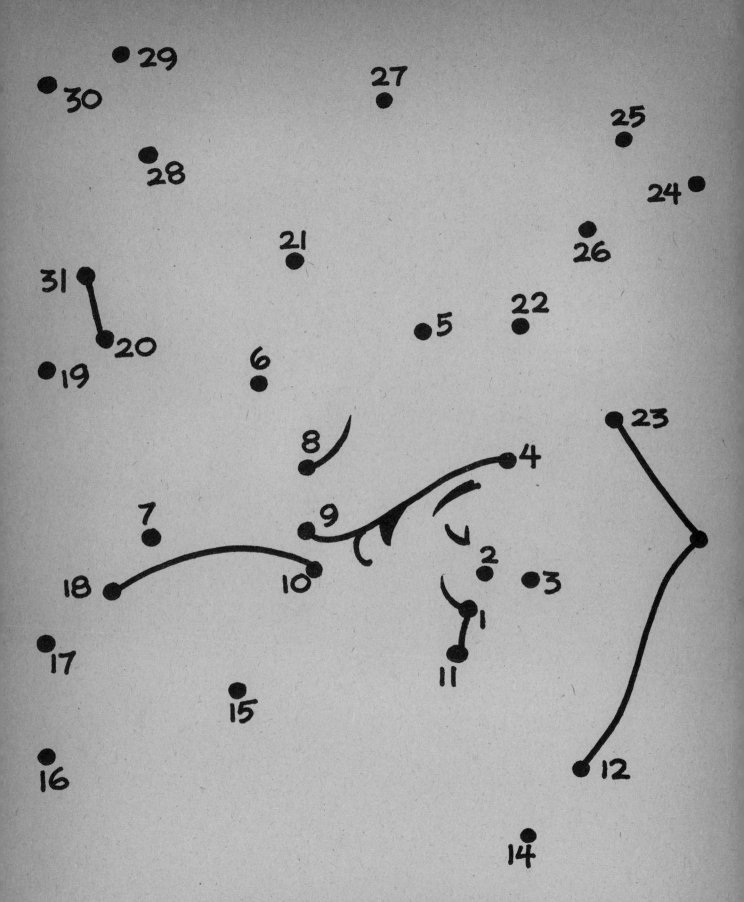

And I in my cap, had just settled
down for a long winter's nap.

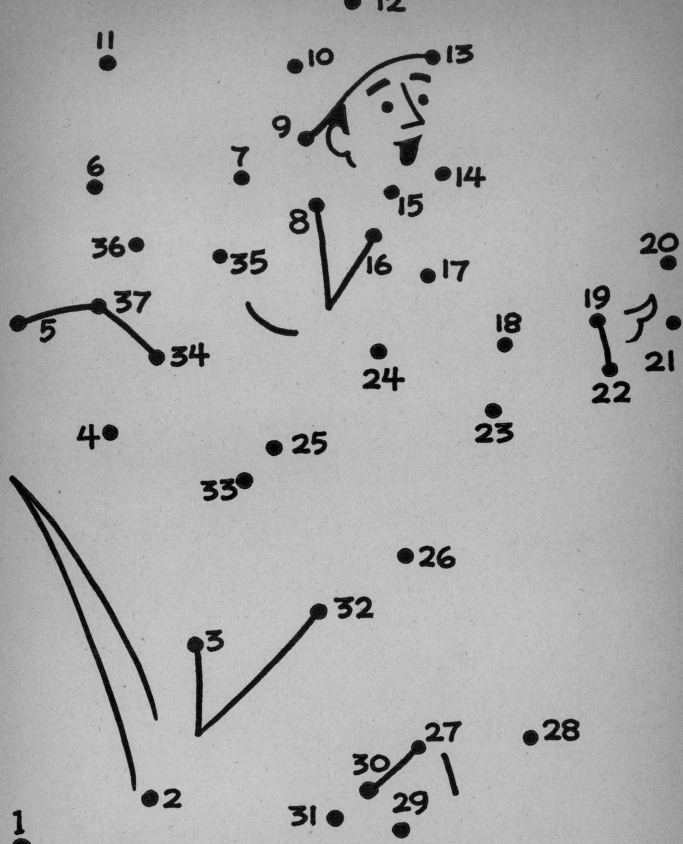

When out on the lawn there arose such a clatter,
I sprang from my bed to see what was the matter.

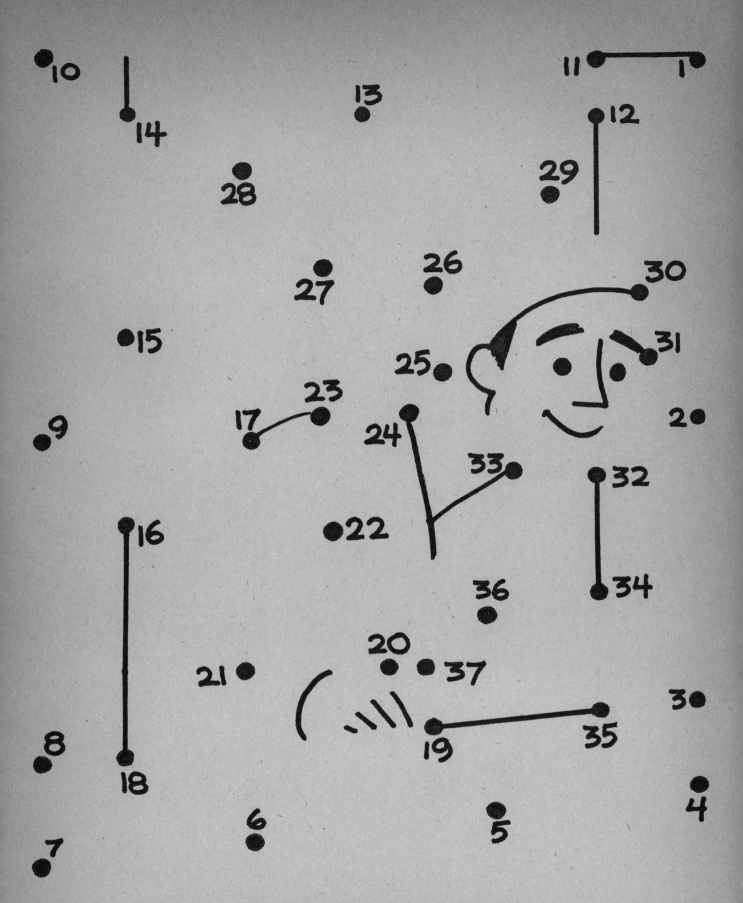

Away to the window I flew like a flash,
tore open the shutters and threw up the sash.

**The moon on the breast of the new-fallen snow,
gave a luster of midday to objects below.**

When, what to my wondering eyes should appear,
but a miniature sleigh and eight tiny reindeer;

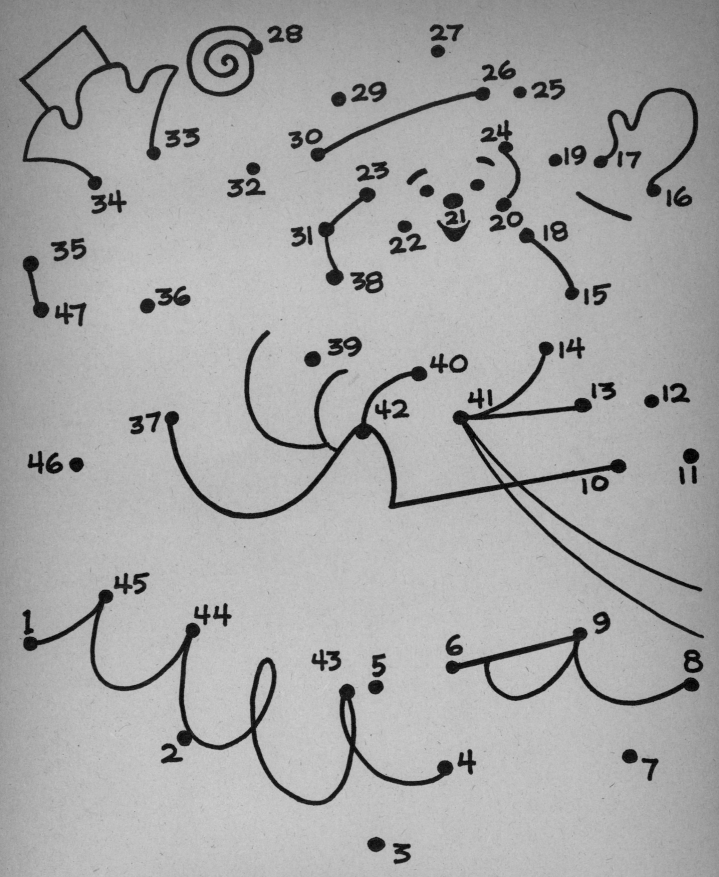

With a little old driver so lively and quick,
I knew in a moment it must be Saint Nick.

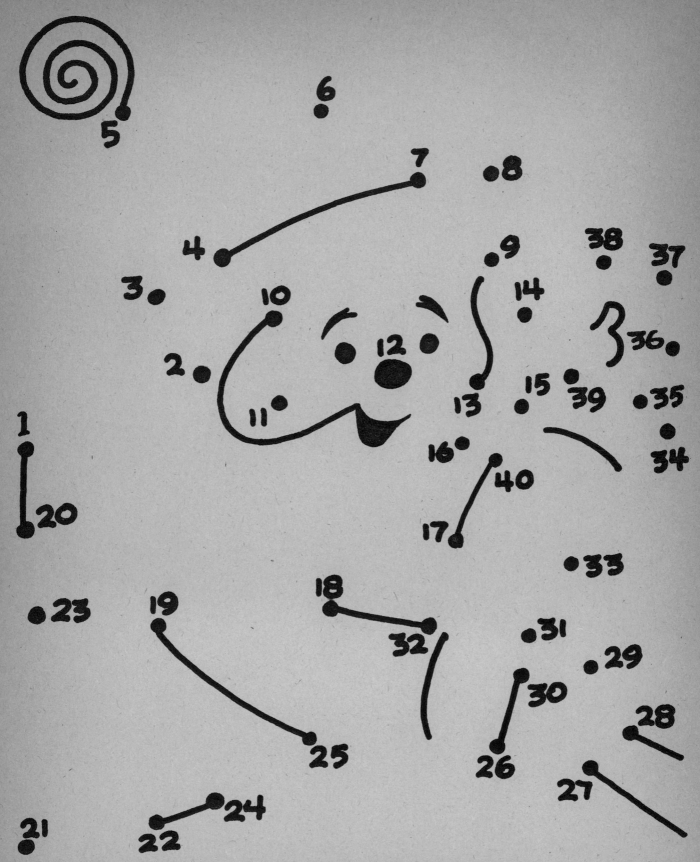

More rapid than eagles his coursers they came,
and he whistled, and shouted, and called them by name:

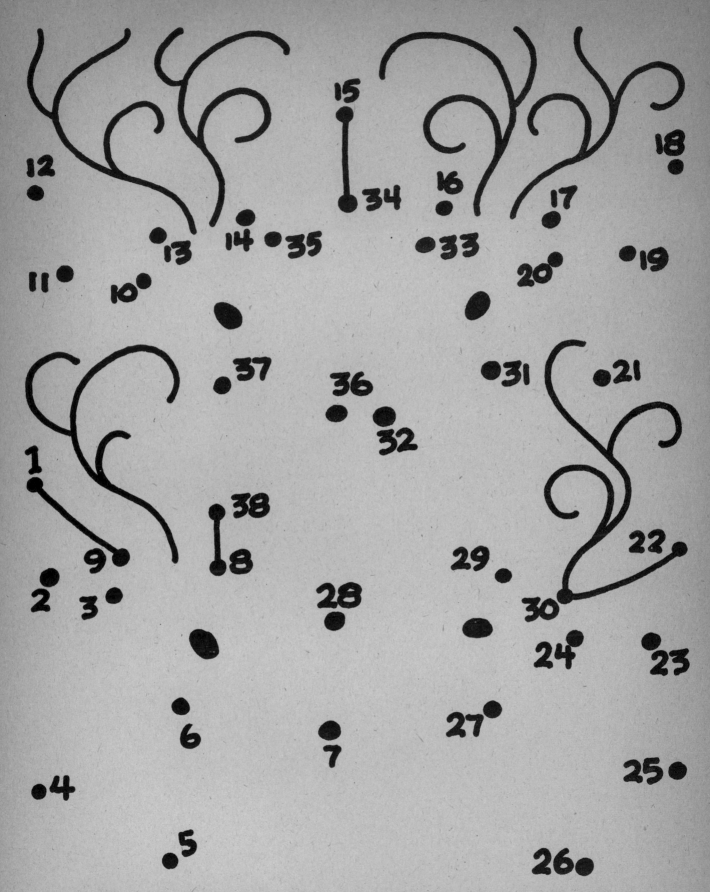

"Now, Dasher! Now, Dancer! Now, Prancer and Vixen!

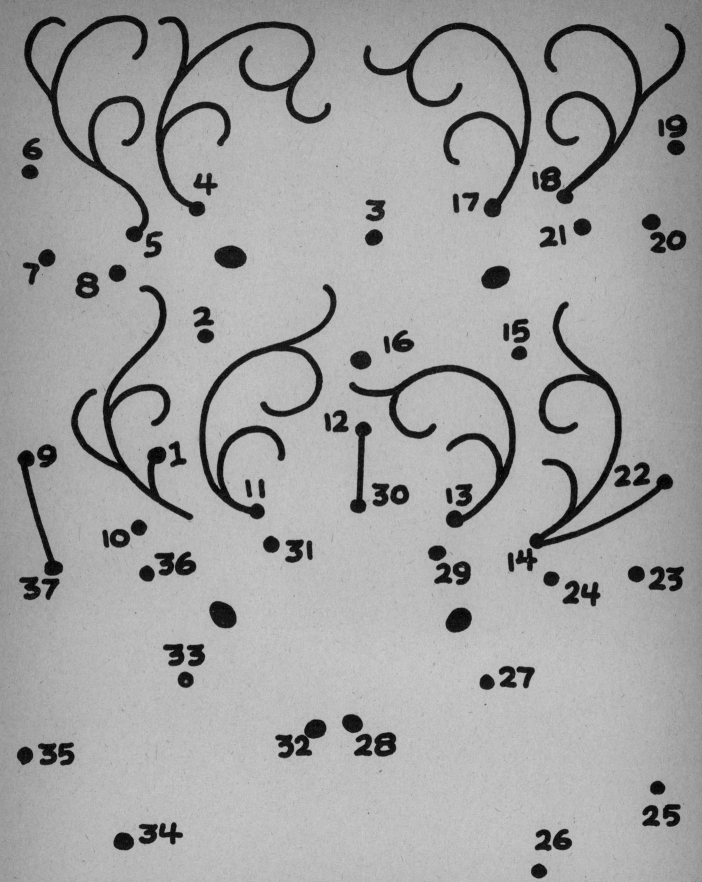

On, Comet! On, Cupid! On, Donner and Blitzen!

To the top of the porch, to the top of the wall!

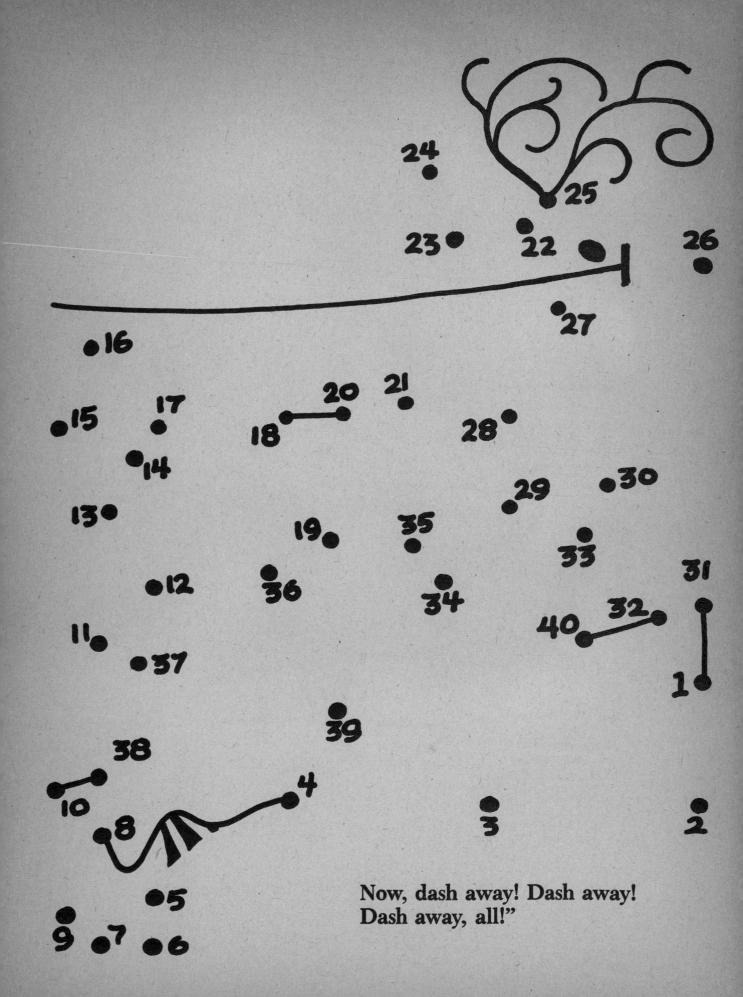

Now, dash away! Dash away!
Dash away, all!"

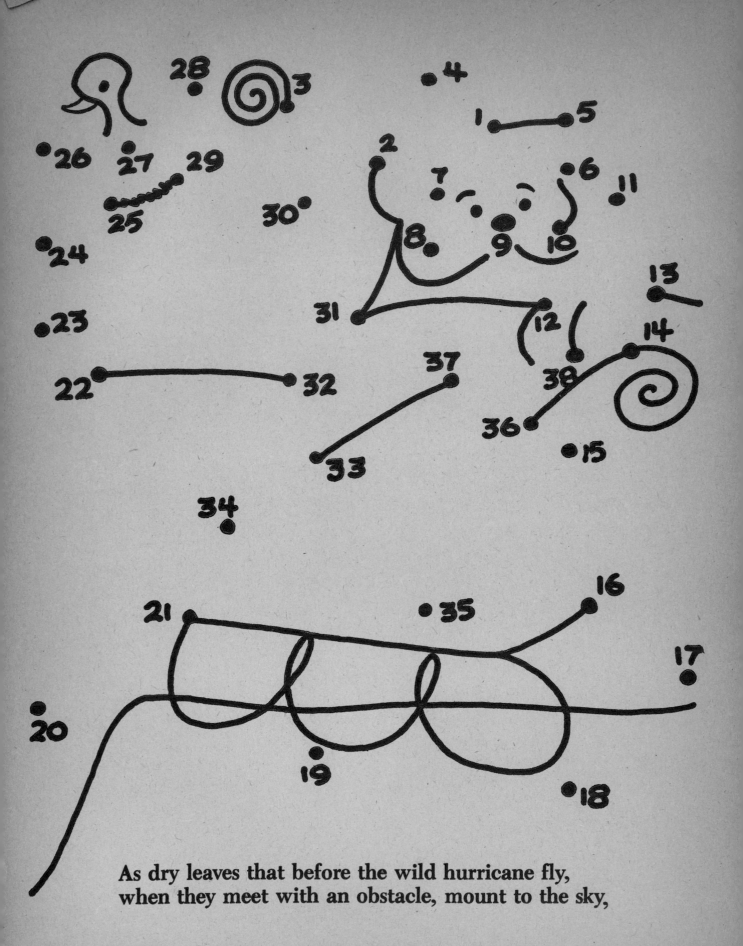

As dry leaves that before the wild hurricane fly,
when they meet with an obstacle, mount to the sky,

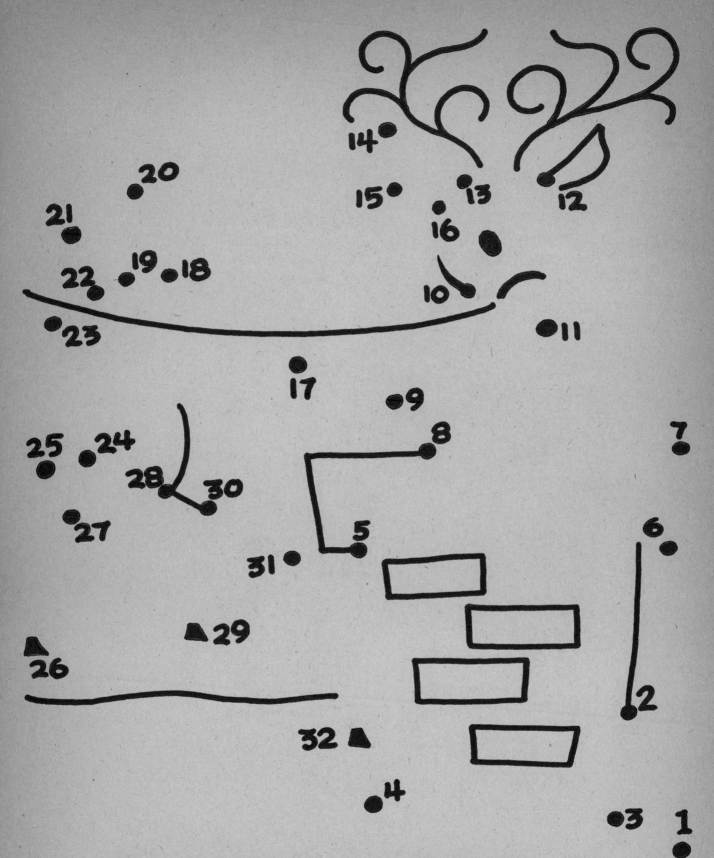

So up to the housetop the coursers they flew
with a sleigh full of toys, and Saint Nicholas, too.

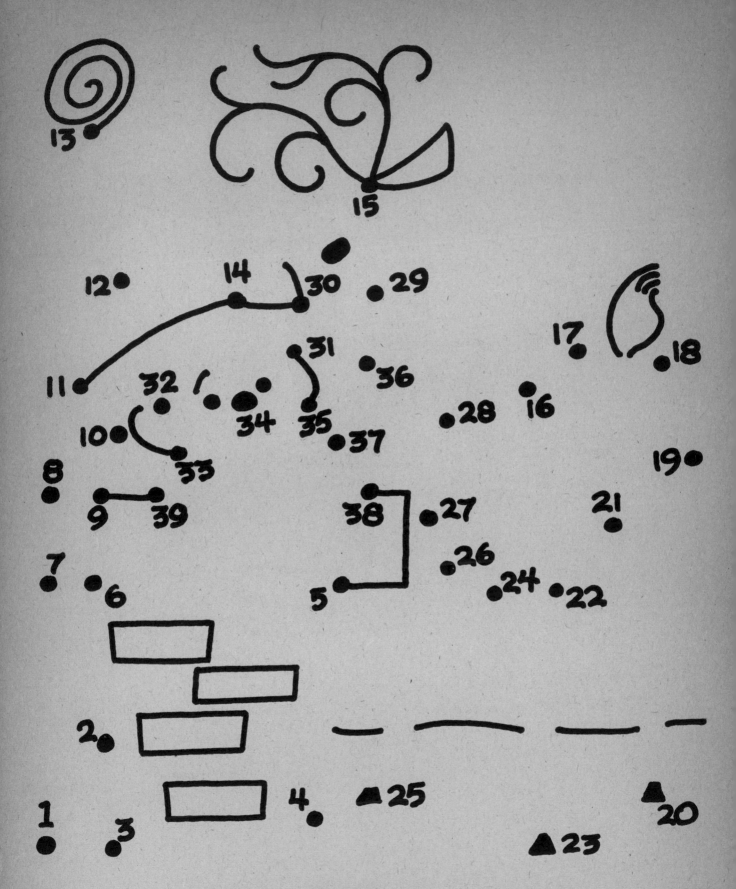

And then in a twinkle, I heard on the roof

The prancing and pawing of each little hoof.

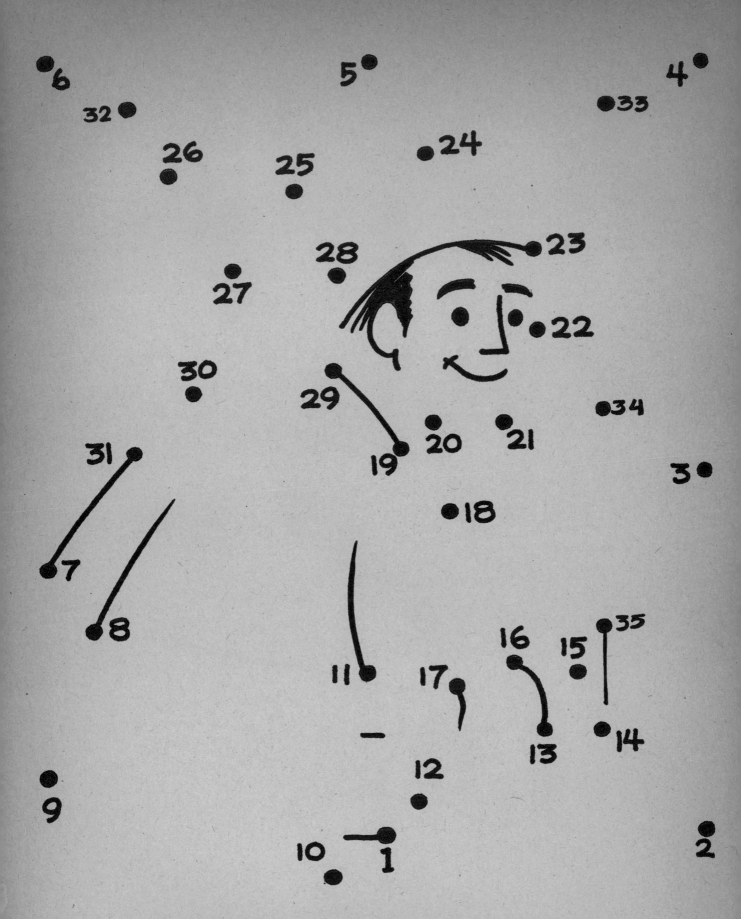

As I drew in my head, and was turning around,

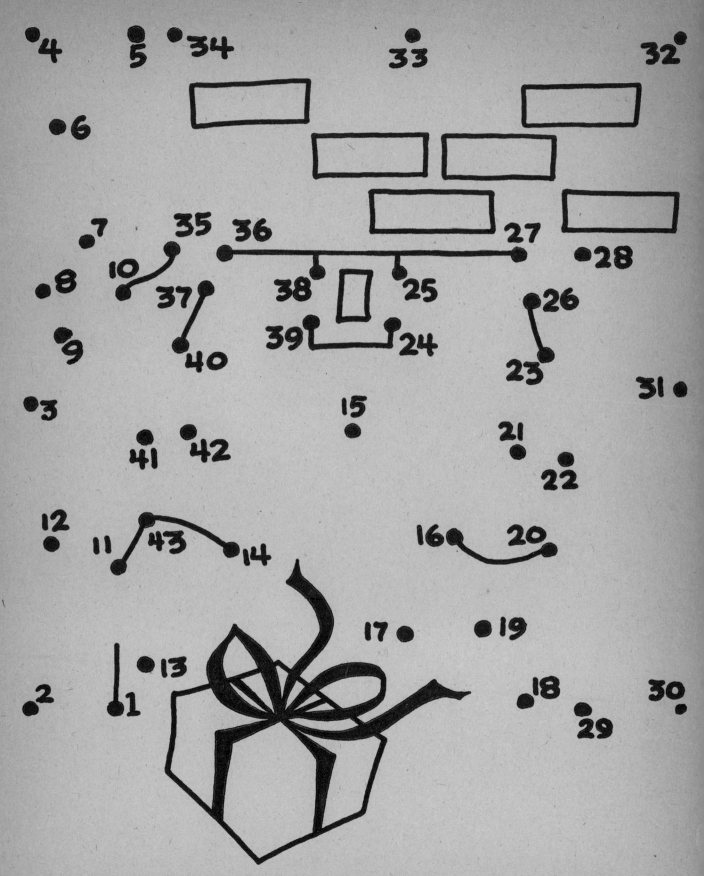

Down the chimney Saint Nicholas came with a bound.

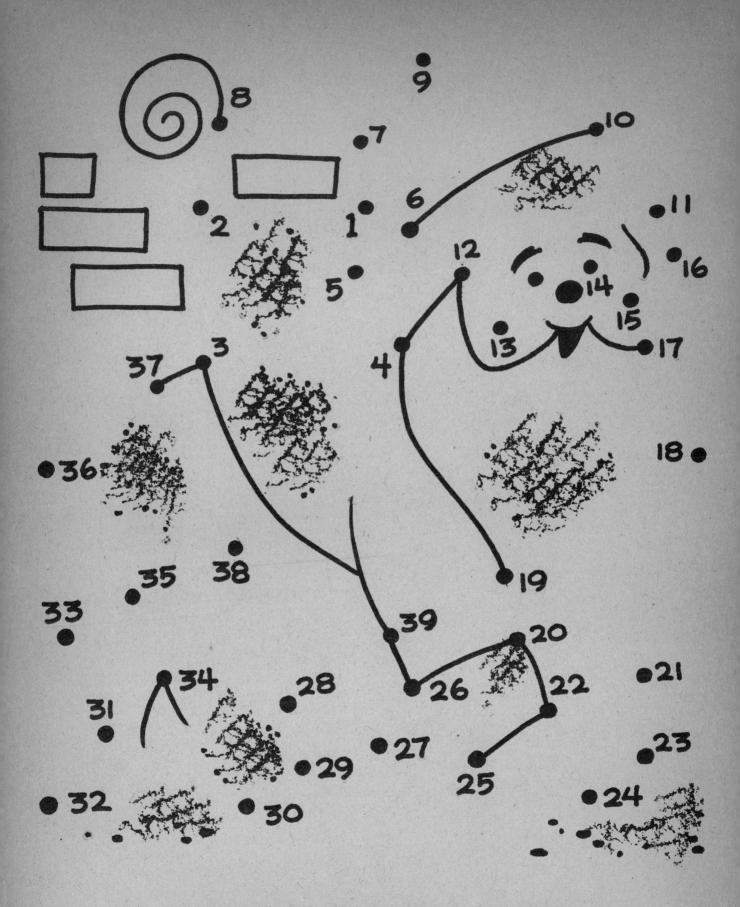

He was dressed all in fur, from his head to his foot,
and his clothes were all tarnished with ashes and soot;

A bundle of toys he had flung on his back,
and he looked like a peddler just opening his pack.

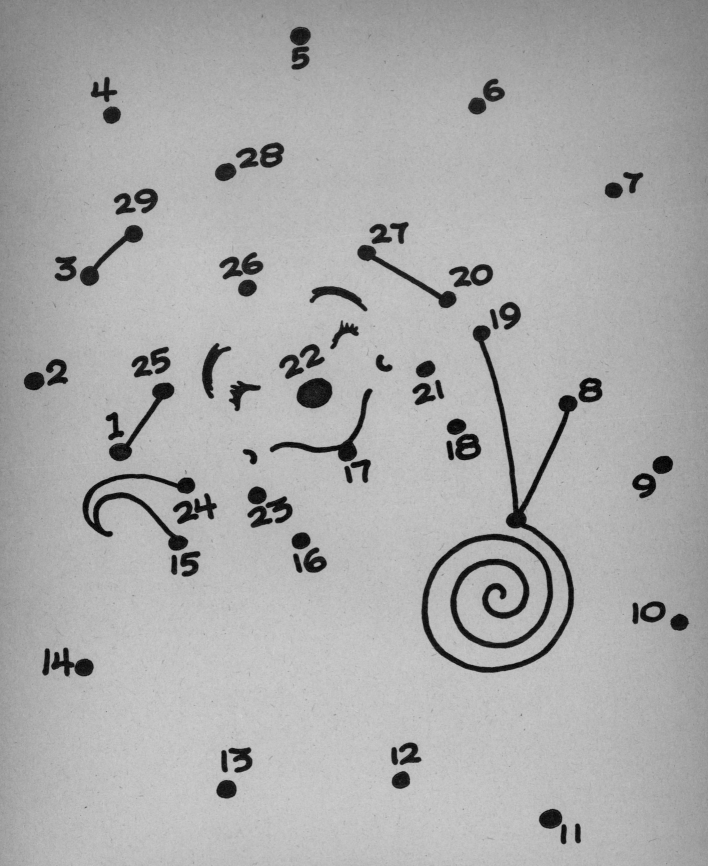

His eyes, how they twinkled! his dimples, how merry!
his cheeks were like roses, his nose like a cherry.

His droll little mouth was drawn up like a bow,
and the beard on his chin was as white as the snow.
The stump of a pipe he held tight in his teeth,
and the smoke, it encircled his head like a wreath.

He had a broad face and a little round belly
that shook when he laughed, like a bowl full of jelly.

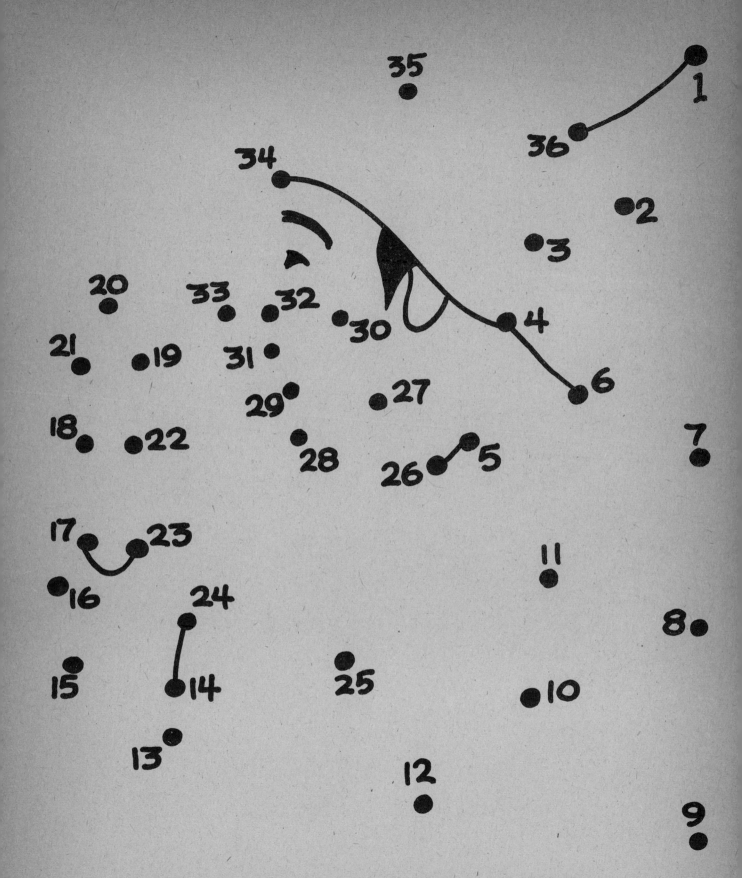

He was chubby and plump, a right jolly old elf,
and I laughed when I saw him, in spite of myself.

A wink of his eye, and a twist of his head
soon gave me to know I had nothing to dread;

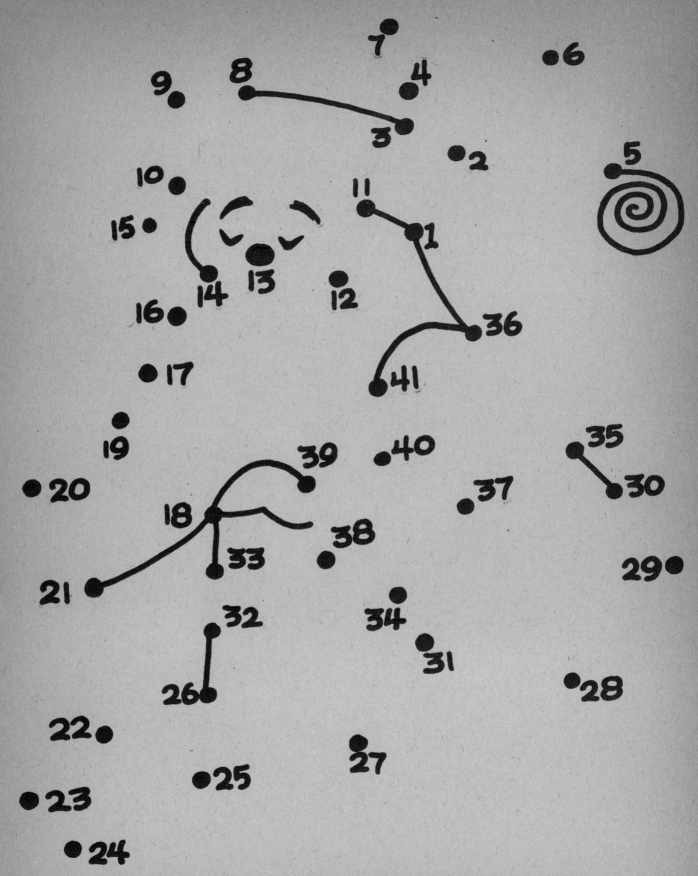

He spoke not a word, but went straight to his work,
and filled all the stockings; then turned with a jerk,

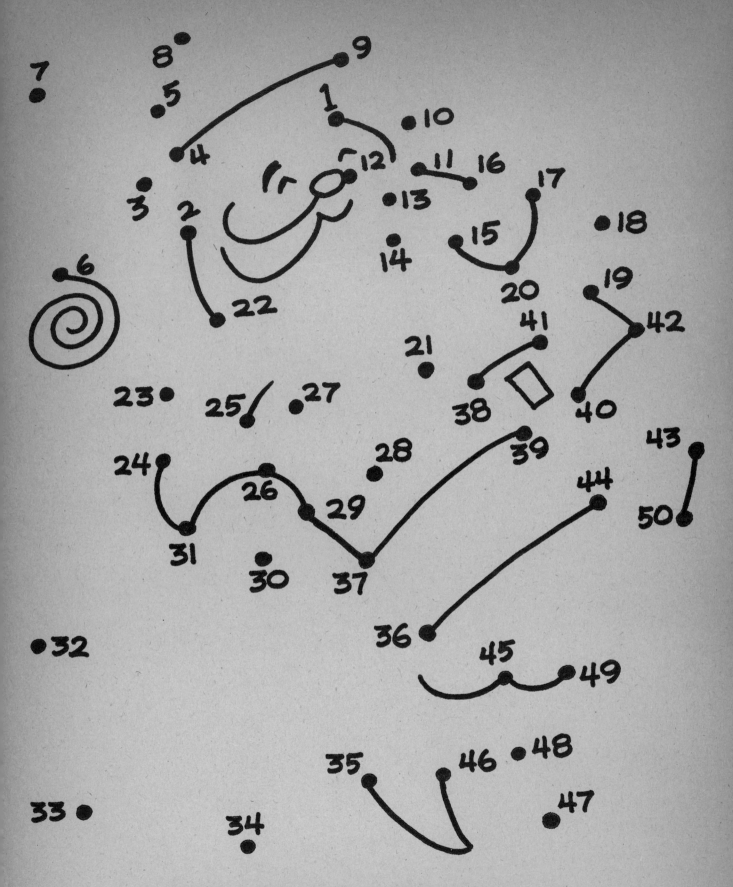

And laying his finger aside of his nose,
and giving a nod, up the chimney he rose.

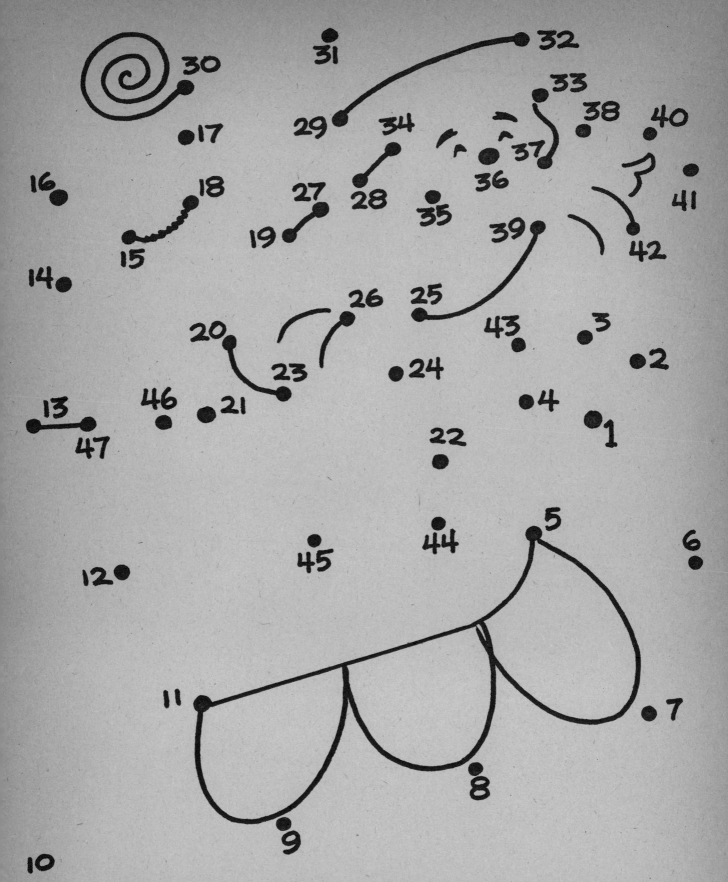

He sprang to his sleigh, to his team gave a whistle,
and away they all flew like the down of a thistle.

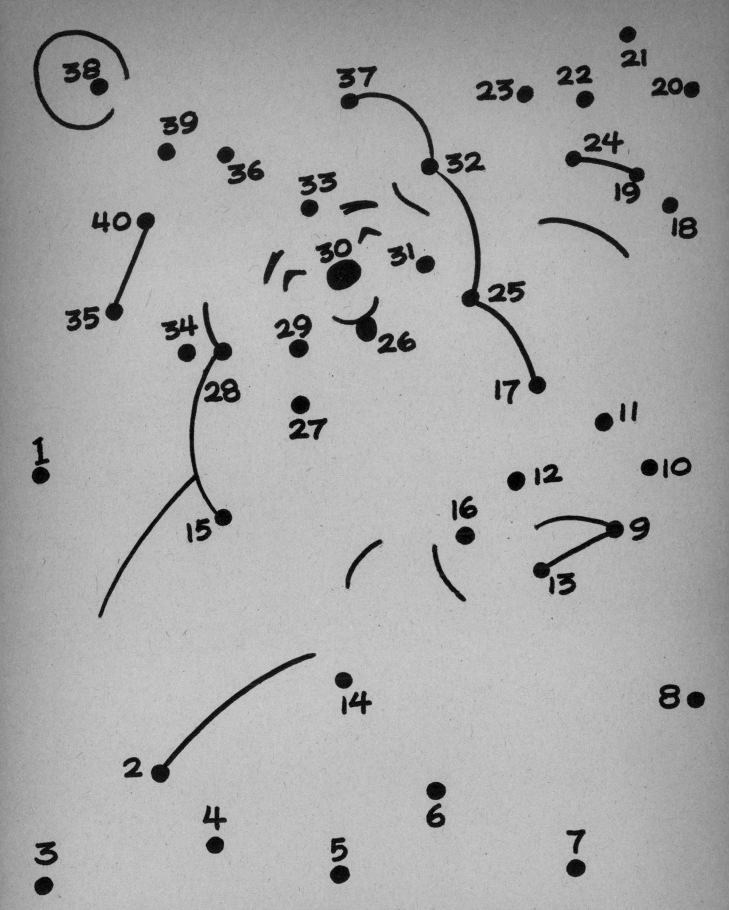

But I heard him exclaim as he drove out of sight,

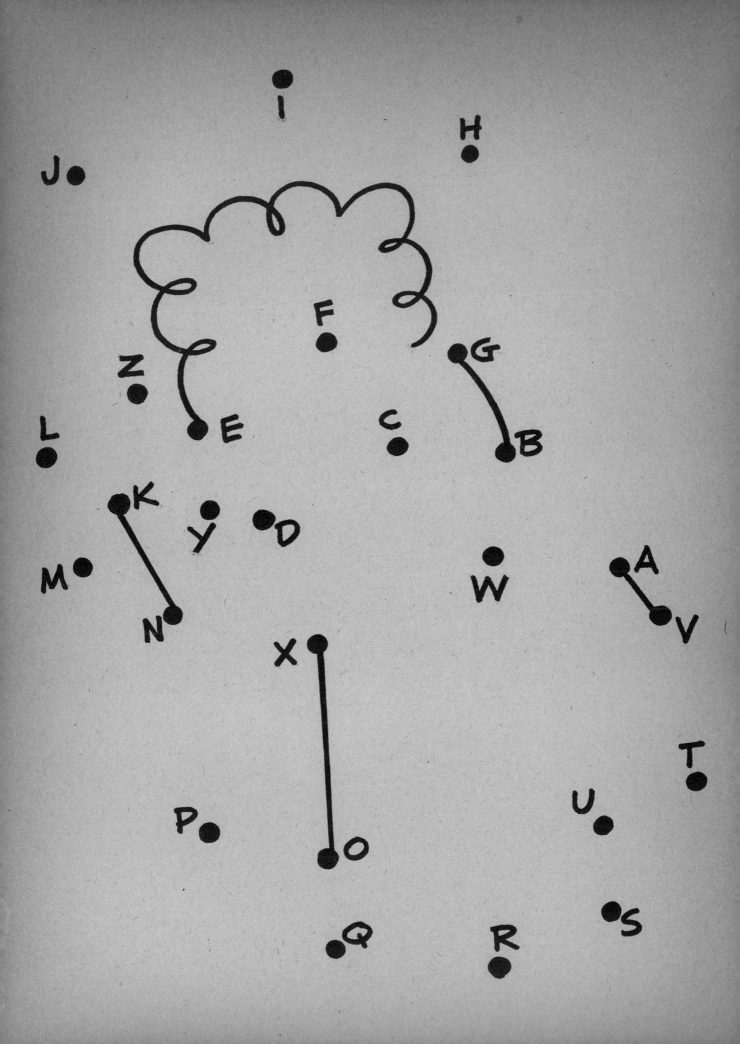

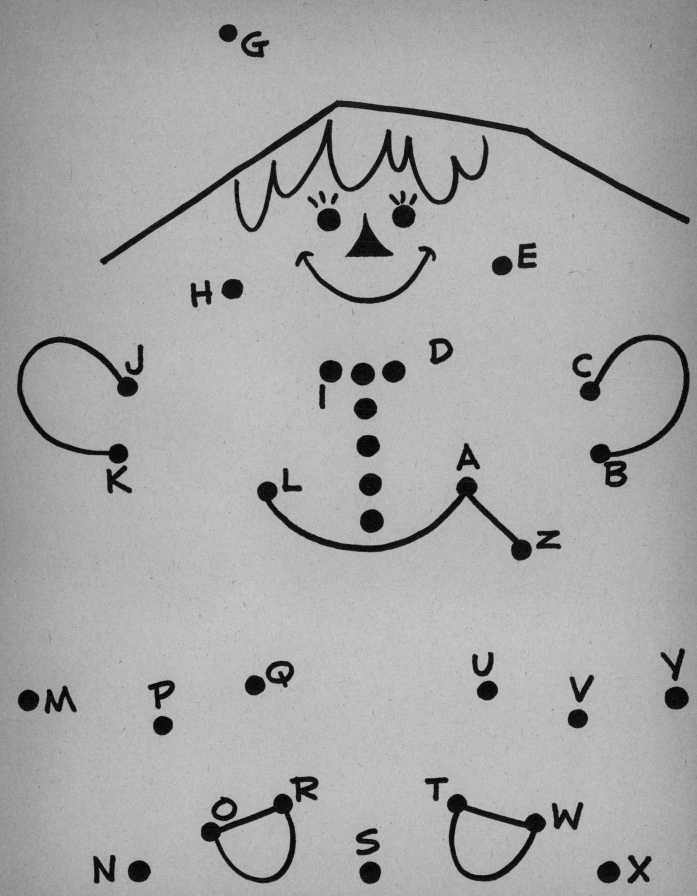

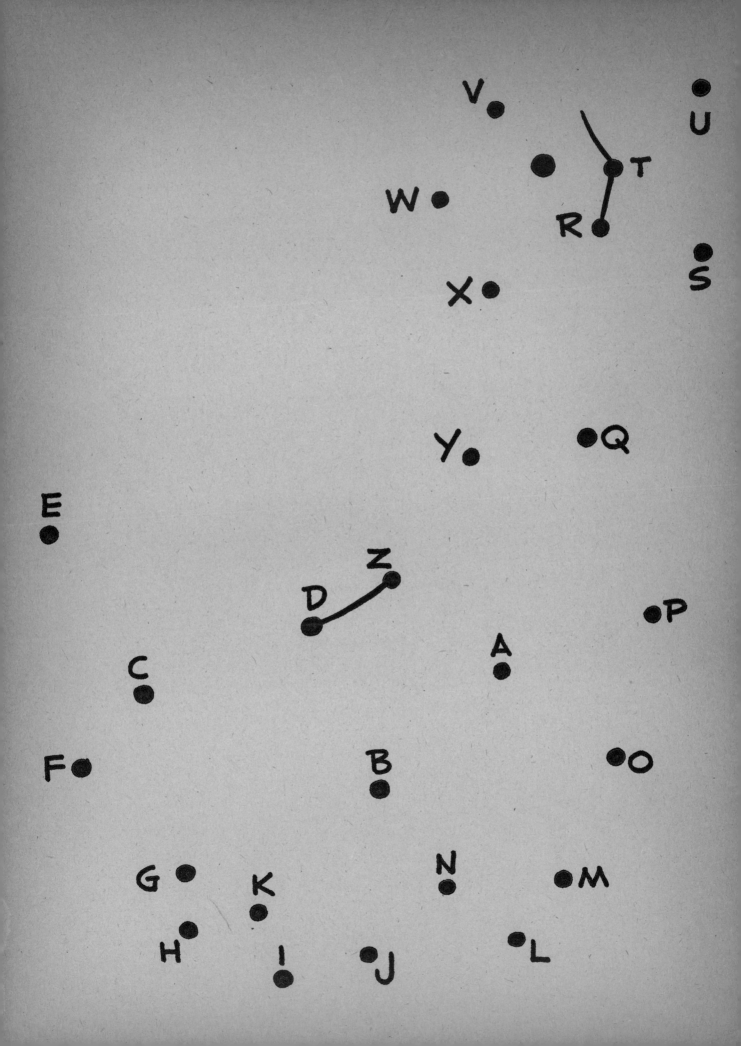

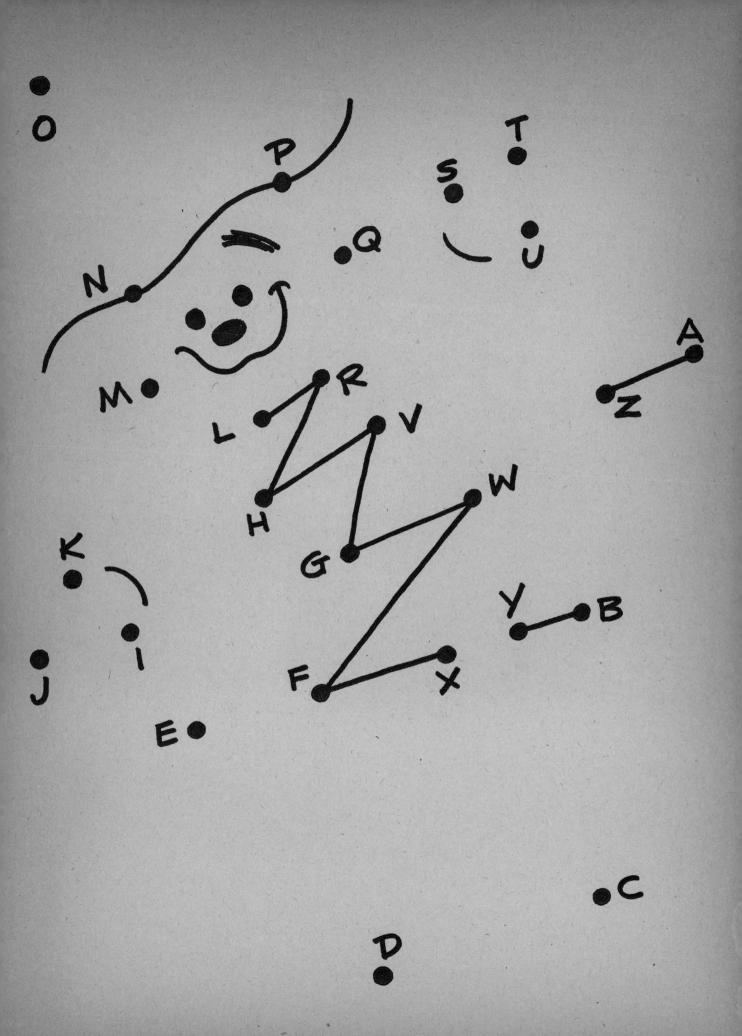

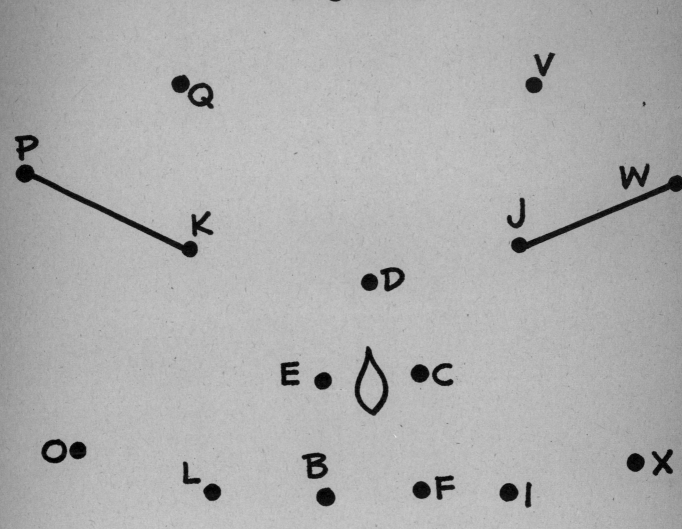

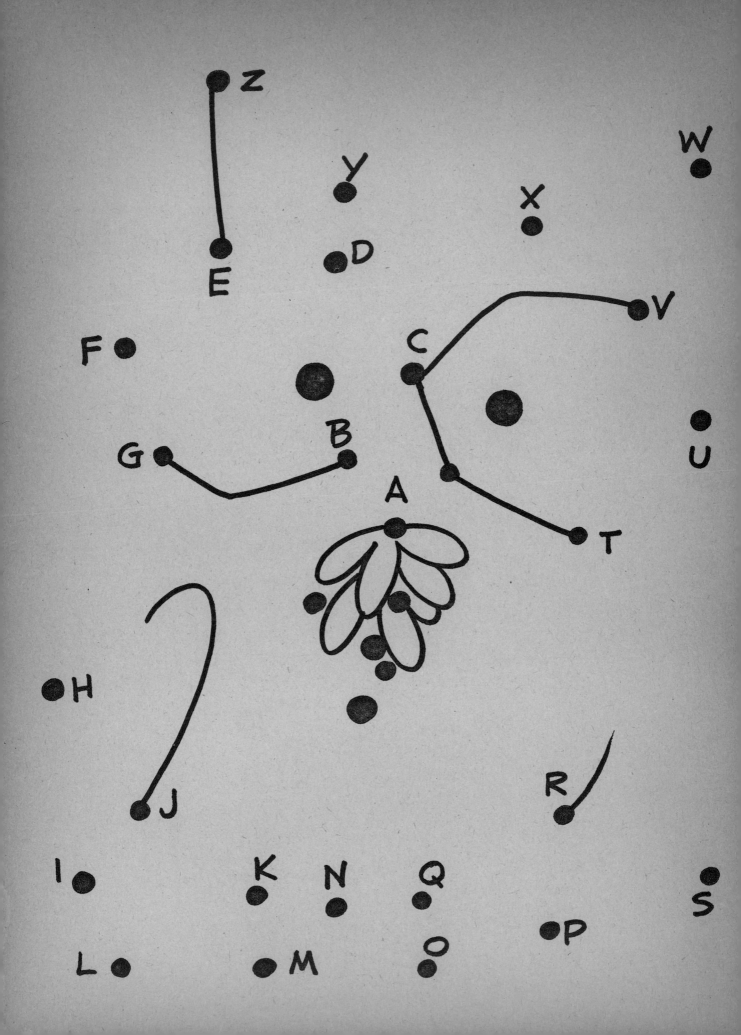

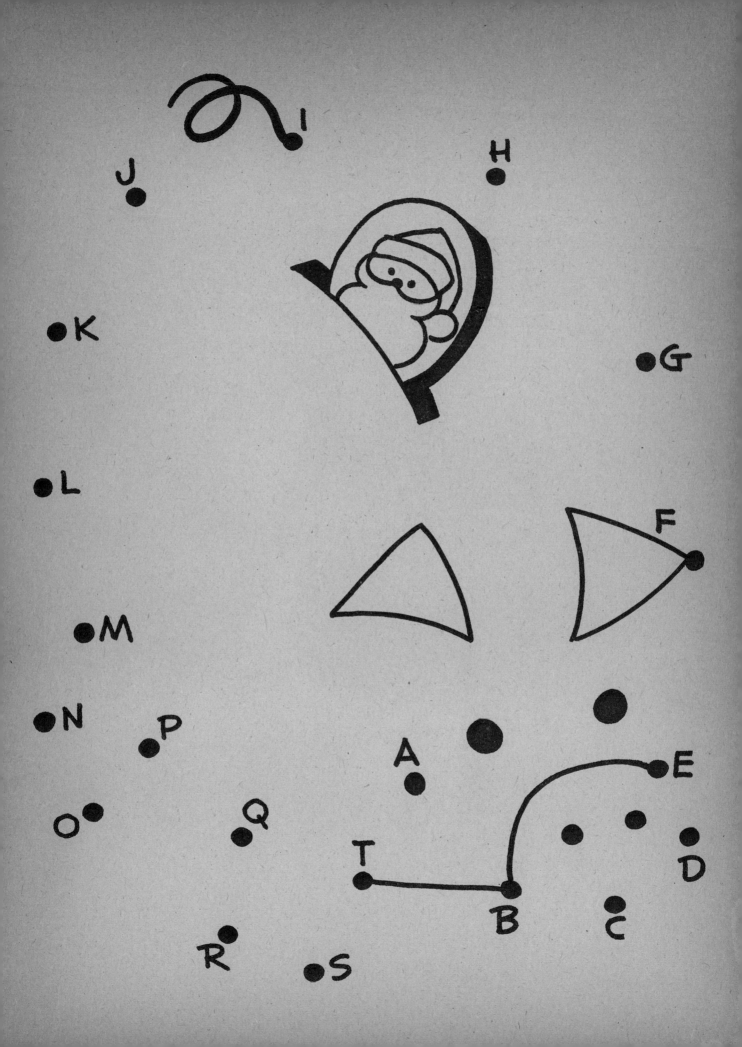

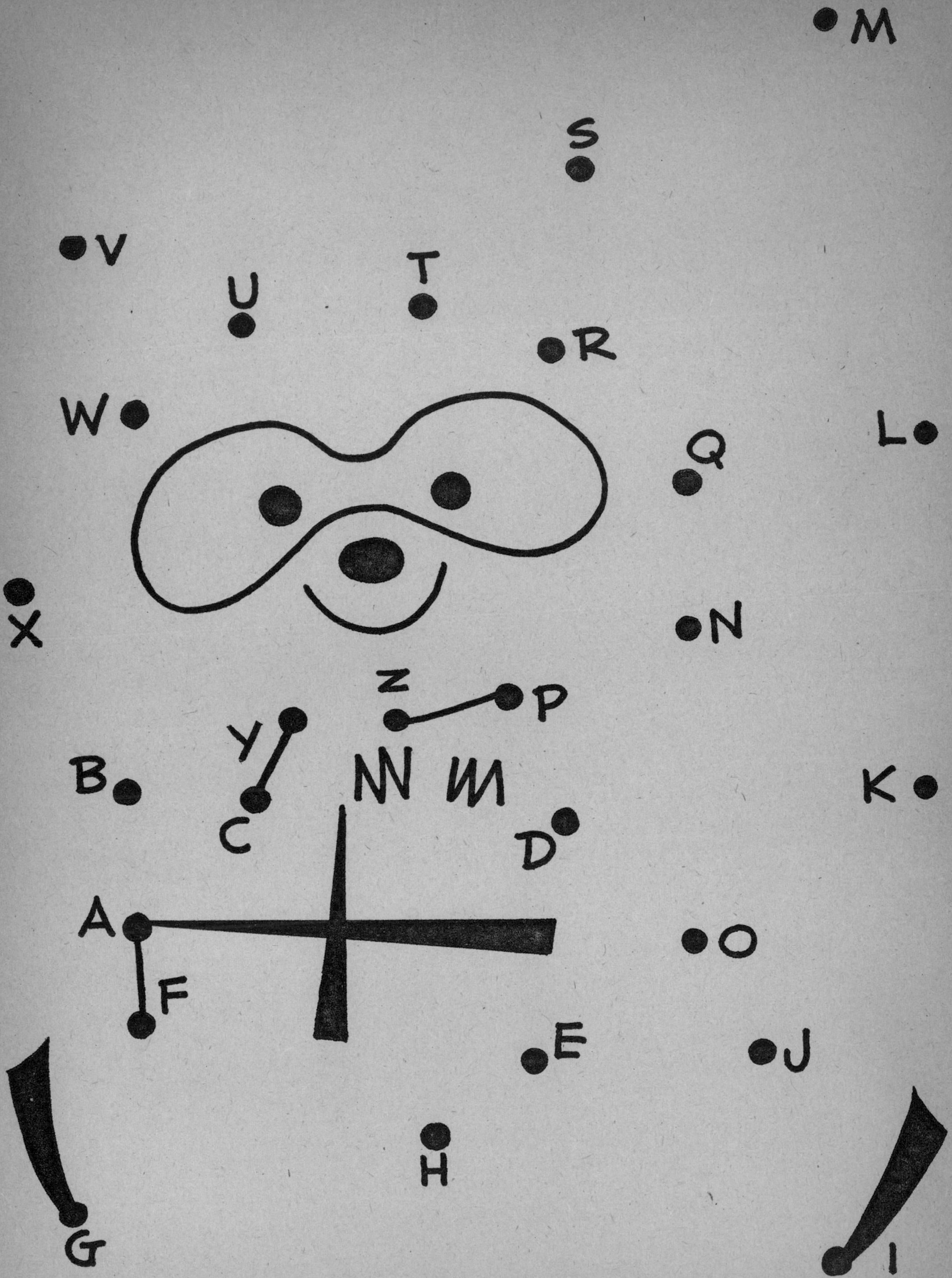
M
S
V
T
U
R
W
L
Q
X
N
Z
P
Y
B
K
C
D
A
O
F
E
J
H
G
I

T

S

R

P

U

Y

N

Q

O

Z

J

V

W

E

X

K

M

D

I

L

F

G

A

H

B

C

•L

•M

K•

J •—• N •O

I•

H •⌣• P

•Q

G•

•R

T•

V•

X•

F•
•Z

•A

•S

U•

E• •Y

W•

D•——•B

•C

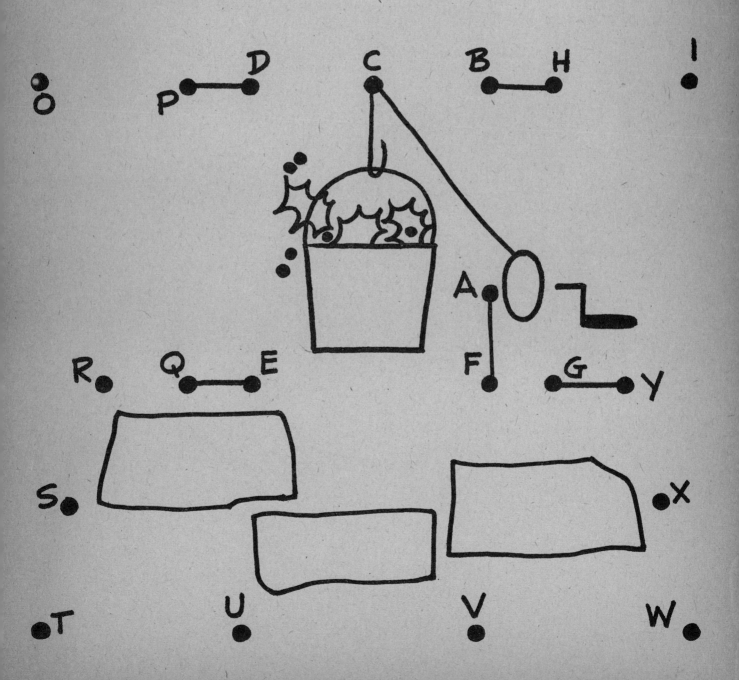

M   L   K

N   J

D   C   B   H   I
P   O

R   Q   E   A   G   Y
                F

S   X

T   U   V   W

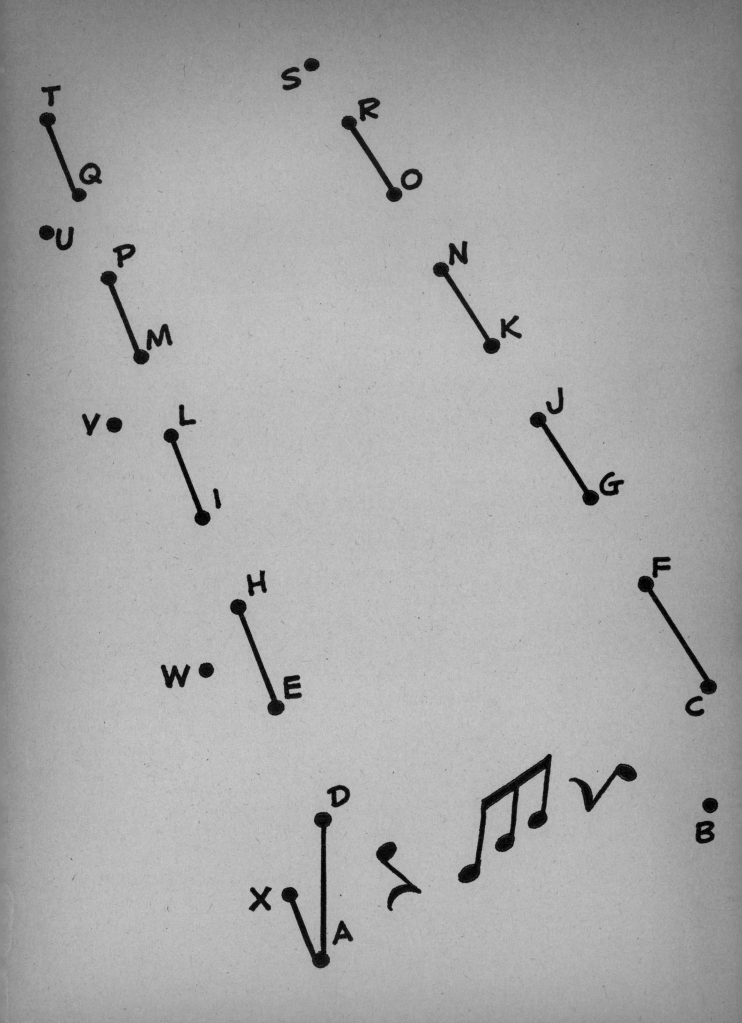

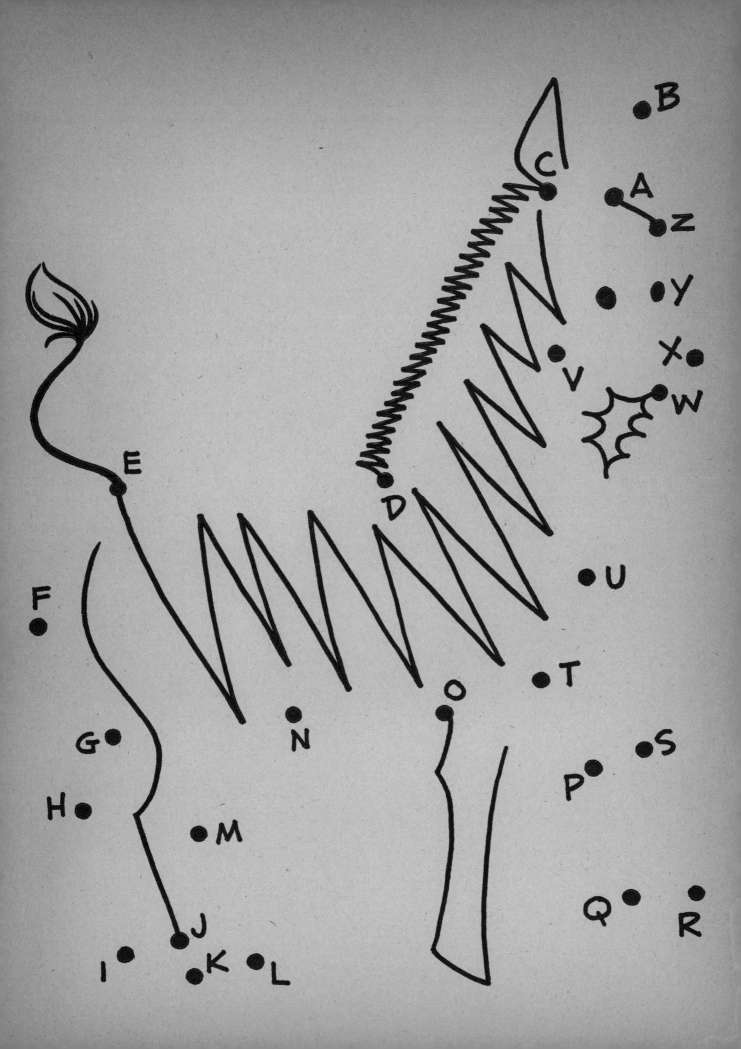

11 ●

12 ●

LIST
MOM
DAD
SIS
GRAM
GRAMP

10 ●

9 ●

2 ●

4 ●

8 ●

3 ●

1

5 ●

6 ●

19 ●

13 ●

7

22 ●

21 ●

20 ●

18 ●

17 ●

16 ●

23 ●

24 ●

15 ●

14 ●

26 ●

25 ●

28

30 ●

27 ●

29 ●